I Want to Be
A POLICE OFFICER

By Liza Alexander
Illustrated by David Prebenna

A SESAME STREET/GOLDEN BOOK
Published by Western Publishing Company, Inc.,
in conjunction with Children's Television Workshop.

© 1994 Children's Television Workshop. Jim Henson's Sesame Street Muppet Characters © 1994 Jim Henson Productions, Inc. All rights reserved. Printed in the U.S.A. No part of this book may be reproduced or copied in any form without written permission from the copyright owner. Sesame Street and the Sesame Street Sign are trademarks and service marks of Children's Television Workshop. All other trademarks are the property of Western Publishing Company, Inc. Library of Congress Catalog Card Number: 93-78574 ISBN: 0-307-13124-6/ISBN: 0-307-63124-9 (lib. bdg.)   MCMXCV

Hi! My name is Herry Monster, and do I have a story for you!

One day Elmo and I were riding our bikes in the park. We were riding fast. We were riding slow. We were zigging. We were zagging. We were having fun.

Suddenly it happened—*crash!* Elmo fell off his bike and onto the hard ground. He began to cry. Oh, no! Elmo had hurt himself.

At first I panicked, but then I remembered what my mommy had told me: "In an emergency, call 911!"

I saw a phone nearby. I rushed over. I picked up the receiver. *Mmmmmmmmm*, went the phone. That was the dial tone, so it was time for me to push in the numbers 9-1-1.

"Hello?" said the operator.

"Herry Monster here," I answered. "I'm calling to report an emergency. Elmo fell off his bike. He might be badly hurt. We're in Sesame Park by the water fountain near the tree that says SARAH LOVES JON."

In no time at all, we heard a siren. *R-R-R-R-r-r-r-r!* A police car zoomed up. Out jumped Police Officer Diaz. She patrols Sesame Street.

She bandaged Elmo's knee and helped him up. She said, "I think your knee is all right, Elmo. Try to walk a little. Herry and I will take you home."

"Elmo feels okey dokey now," said Elmo.

Then we put the bikes into the trunk of the police car and took Elmo home.

I said to Officer Diaz, "Helping people makes me feel strong and brave!"

She laughed and said, "Then you feel just like a police officer! Would you like to join me on patrol today?"

"Wow, thanks!" I said. "I sure would!"

Off we sped on patrol, and we found a big exciting parade!

"It's a motorcade," said Officer Diaz. "Someone very important must be visiting Sesame Street."

Our important visitor was riding in a big black limousine. Police officers on horses rode behind the limo and beside it. In front were officers on motorcycles. *Vroom! Vroom!*

We followed the motorcade and learned that our important visitor was the First Lady of the United States! She is married to the President. The First Lady had come to meet the kids on Sesame Street.

Officer Diaz introduced me to a policeman on a horse. Officer Travis is his name, and he let me pet his horse, whose name is Chrissie.

Chrissie is a police horse, but just like any other horse, she likes carrots! Officer Travis gave me one to feed her.

Officer Travis wore high shiny boots and a special riding helmet. He looked really spiffy.

I asked, "How did you become a policeman, Officer Travis?"

"After high school I went to the police academy," he explained. "It's a special school where students learn to be officers. When you're old enough, you could go there, too, Herry."

And I said, "Really? Think of that! Wow!"

Then Officer Diaz took me to the Police Station. She said, "Herry, meet a very special officer!"

Well, you could have knocked me over with a feather. The very special officer was a police dog named Willy!

His partner was named Officer Loredo. She said, "Willy goes everywhere with me. He uses his keen nose and ears to help me in my police work."

Officer Loredo showed us the police scooter that she and Willy ride around town. Willy sits right there on the front seat next to Officer Loredo. One of the few things Willy doesn't know how to do is drive!

Officer Diaz and I took off on patrol again. We got a call from the station house on the car radio. The call said, "Lost child at Sesame and Vine."

R-R-R-R-r r r r! We zoomed through the streets!

Sure enough, at the corner of Sesame and Vine was a little lost monster.

"I want my mommy!" he cried. "I want to go home!"

Officer Diaz held the little monster's hand. She asked his name. He said it was Max.

"Where did you last see your mommy?" asked Officer Diaz.

"I don't remember!" said Max. He was still crying.

Officer Diaz calmed Max down. "Where did you get that ice cream cone, sweetheart?" she asked.

"I don't remember!" said Max, crying.

Then Officer Diaz said, "There, there, Max, it's all right. May I look at your napkin?"

The napkin said HOOPER'S STORE!

We hurried to Hooper's. There was Max's mommy!
Max had wandered out the door by himself when she
wasn't looking.

Max's mommy was so glad to find her son that she
hugged all of us, even Officer Diaz!

We were happy for Max and his mommy. And now it was time to take a break.

We sat down, and I tried on Officer Diaz's hat and badge. She said, "Herry, my hat and badge suit you nicely."

"Terrific!" I said. "Because when I grow up, I want to be a police officer!"